Mrs. Tiggy-Winkle

Retold by
Sarah Toast

Book illustrated by
Sam Thiewes
and
Pat Schoonover

Cover illustrated by
Anita Nelson

Based on the original story by Beatrix Potter with all new illustrations.

Louis Weber, C.E.O.
Publications International, Ltd.
7373 North Cicero Avenue
Lincolnwood, Illinois 60646

Manufactured in U.S.A.

8 7 6 5 4 3 2 1

ISBN: 0-7853-1146-7

PUBLICATIONS INTERNATIONAL, LTD.
Little Rainbow is a trademark of Publications International, Ltd.

Once upon a time there was a little girl named Lucie who lived on a farm. She was a good little girl, but she was always losing things.

One day Lucie came crying into the farmyard, "Oh! I've lost another handkerchief! Now that makes three handkerchiefs and a pinafore lost! Have you seen them, Tabby Kitten?"

Tabby Kitten just went on washing her white paws, so Lucie asked the hen, "Sally Henny-Penny, have you found my handkerchiefs?" The hen just ran off clucking.

Lucie turned and looked up at the hill behind the farm. Way up on the hillside she thought she saw something white spread out on the grass.

Lucie went through the farmyard gate and scrambled up the steep path. She ran up and up until she could see the farm far below.

The path ended under a big rock. Lucie saw clotheslines of braided grass wound around sticks and a heap of tiny clothespins on the ground.

There was something else—a door straight into the hill!

Lucie knocked on the door, and a voice called out, "Who's that?"

Lucie opened the door and went into a nice, clean farm kitchen. But the ceiling was so low that Lucie's head nearly bumped it. Everything in that kitchen was small!

At the table stood a very short, round person with an iron in her hand. She had a little black nose that went sniffle, sniffle, snuffle and eyes that went twinkle, twinkle. Underneath her ruffled cap, that little person had prickles instead of curls!

"Who are you?" asked Lucie. "Have you seen my handkerchiefs?"

The little person replied, "Oh, yes, miss. My name is Mrs. Tiggy-Winkle." She then pulled something out of the clothes basket and spread it over the table for Lucie to see.

"That's one of my handkerchiefs!" cried Lucie. "And there's my pinafore!"

Then Mrs. Tiggy-Winkle ironed Lucie's pinafore. She took special care to impress Lucie.

"Oh my, isn't that lovely!" said Lucie gratefully.

Mrs. Tiggy-Winkle fetched something else out of the basket.

"Why look, another handkerchief, but it's red!" said Lucie.

"If you please, this one belongs to Mrs. Rabbit," said Mrs. Tiggy-Winkle. She ironed the red handkerchief, then a little red vest for Cock Robin and a tablecloth for Jenny Wren. Then she pulled out a blue jacket belonging to Peter Rabbit.

In the bottom of the basket were more of Lucie's handkerchiefs, which Mrs. Tiggy-Winkle ironed.

Then Mrs. Tiggy-Winkle made tea for herself and Lucie. They sat on a bench in front of the fire to talk and drink their tea.

Lucie noticed some small prickles sticking out of Mrs. Tiggy-Winkle's cap and gown, so she didn't want to sit too near her.

When they had finished their tea, they tied up the freshly ironed clothes in tidy bundles. They folded up Lucie's handkerchiefs inside her clean pinafore, and they fastened the bundle with a silver safety pin.

Lucie and Mrs. Tiggy-Winkle trotted down the hill with the bundles of clothes. All the way along the path, little animals and birds came out to meet them. The very first animals that they met were Peter Rabbit and his friend Benjamin Bunny.

Mrs. Tiggy-Winkle gave Peter Rabbit his little blue coat, and she gave Benjamin Bunny the red handkerchief to give to old Mrs. Rabbit. Every one of the little animals was very grateful to dear Mrs. Tiggy-Winkle for washing and ironing their clothes.

Lucie and Mrs. Tiggy-Winkle continued to walk down the hill. There was nothing left to carry except Lucie's one little bundle.

When they reached the bottom of the hill they stopped at the gate to the farmyard. Mrs. Tiggy-Winkle said that Lucie must be sure to stop by some day soon for another cup of tea.

Lucie went through the gate with her bundle, then she returned to say thank-you and good-bye to the little washerwoman who had prickles under her cap.

But what a very odd thing! Mrs. Tiggy-Winkle had not waited for thanks or payment! She was running, running, running up the hill.

Where was her white ruffled cap? Where was her lovely fringed shawl? And where were her print gown and striped petticoat?

And how small she now seemed, and how brown—and she was covered with prickles!

Why, Mrs. Tiggy-Winkle, as it turned out, was nothing but a roly-poly little hedgehog!

Some people say that Lucie must have been napping and dreaming by the farmyard gate. But if that was so, how could she have found three clean handkerchiefs and a pinafore, all pinned with a silver safety pin?

And besides, others have seen that door into the back of the hill.